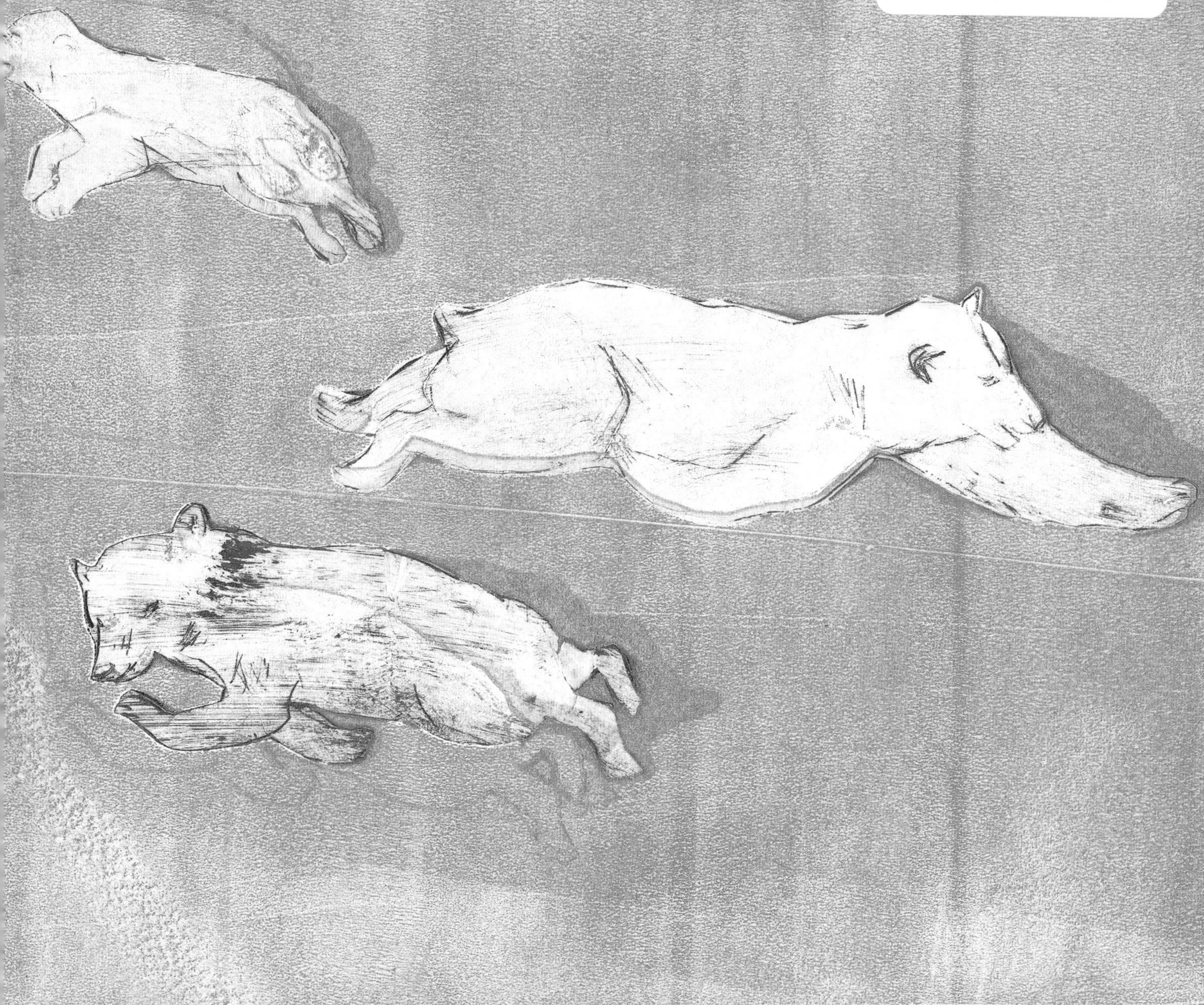

Manufactured in China, June 2013
This product conforms to CPSIA 2008

Library of Congress Cataloging-in-Publication Data is available on file.

ISBN: 978-1-62087-985-6

Written by Alessandro Lecis • Illustrated by Linda Wolfsgruber
Translated from the German by Talia Rebecca Ergas

I Am NOT
Little Red Riding Hood

Sky Pony Press • New York

I am not Little Red Riding Hood.

But I wore a red scarf and took a basket into the woods.

I am not Little Red
Riding Hood, and I
didn't meet a big bad wolf
in the woods. Instead, I
met a white bear.

"What are you carrying
in your basket?" asked the
bear.

"Nothing. I'm collecting snow, soft snow: whiter than milk, fluffier than the clouds, and fresher than vanilla ice cream."

"Impossible," said the bear. "You can play and dance in the snow, but you can't take it with you."

"Look up there," said the bear, "where the moon
hangs in the sky. There you will find snow fluffier
than the clouds, whiter than milk, and fresher than
vanilla ice cream. There the moon lies sleeping,
getting its white color. Come, sit on my back,
and I'll take you there."

With me on his back, the bear
plodded through the woods. Soon
I fell asleep, gently rocking
on his shoulders.

"Wake up, we're here," said the bear. "It's time to dance."
So we danced the snow dance, and the snowflakes
swirled around us—fresher than vanilla ice cream,
fluffier than the clouds, and whiter than milk. I was a
snowflake among many, and the bear was white as snow.

I collected snow in my basket until it was full,
and the bear ate as many snowflakes as he could.

This bear was quite strange.
Where did he come from? I wondered.
He plucked snowflakes from the sky
and was as happy as could be.

As my basket and his belly became full, the bear said,
"It's almost dawn. Let me take you home."

When we arrived, I gave
the bear my red scarf.
"Where is your home?" I asked him.
The bear didn't answer. He just
plodded away. I watched him until his
white fur disappeared in the snow.

I looked into my basket and it was empty.
The bear was right: I could look at the snow,
I could play and dance in the snow,
but I could not keep the snow.

I am not Little Red Riding Hood,
and I did not meet a big bad wolf in the woods.
There was no grandmother and no hunter, but instead a white bear.
A bear that danced in the snow and ate as many snowflakes
as he could, where the moon lies sleeping.

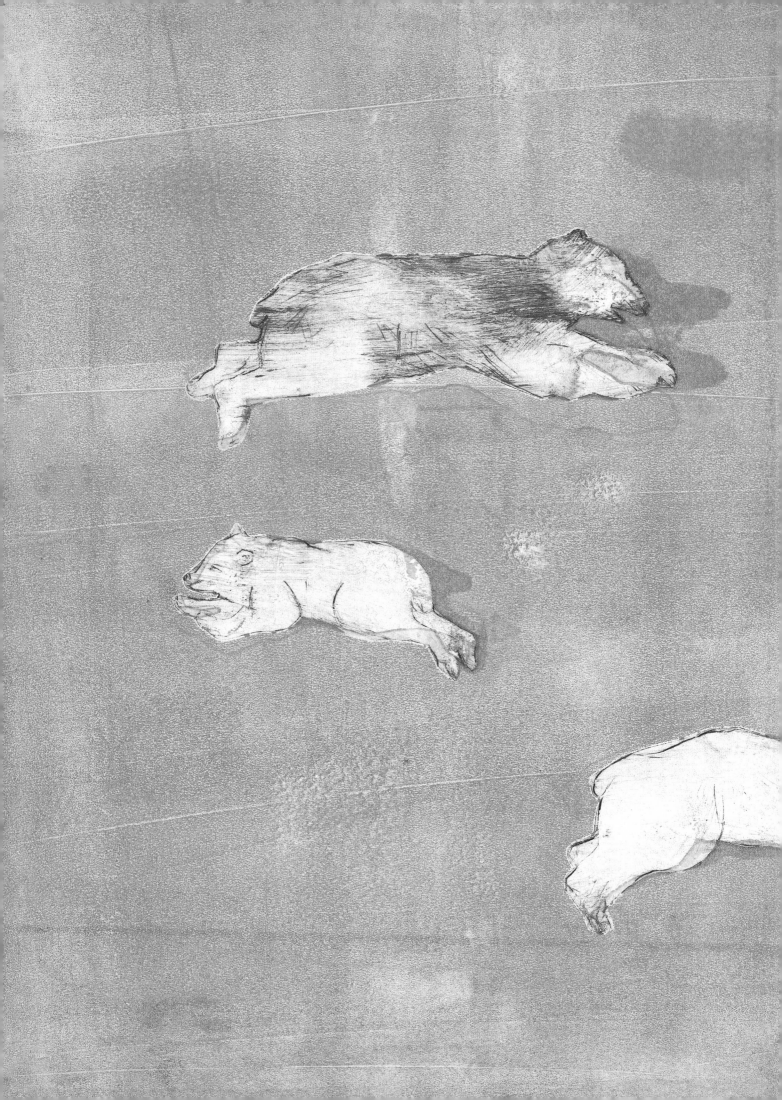